Everybody counts!

D1307057

The day Anthony Counted to a Googol

A story by Mark North
Illustrated by Mark Stephen Ross

ISBN-13: 9780615295572
Published in Nashville, TN by Mark North Publications
Printed in the United States of America

To Anthony, Karly, and Lara:
Keep on counting!

When Anthony was a little boy,
he would walk around counting to himself
all day and into the night.

1

He didn't play.

He didn't watch TV.

He didn't even notice that everyone
in the family was watching.

He just kept on counting.

After several days of counting, he reached numbers
that were so high he had to ask his Uncle Stephen
what came next.

"A million,"
Uncle Stephen answered.

"A billion"

was the answer the next time.

And Anthony kept on counting.

One day, Uncle Stephen told Anthony
about the number googol. No one else in the family
believed there was a number googol but they were wrong.

There really is a number googol.
It is a very large number. It looks like this:

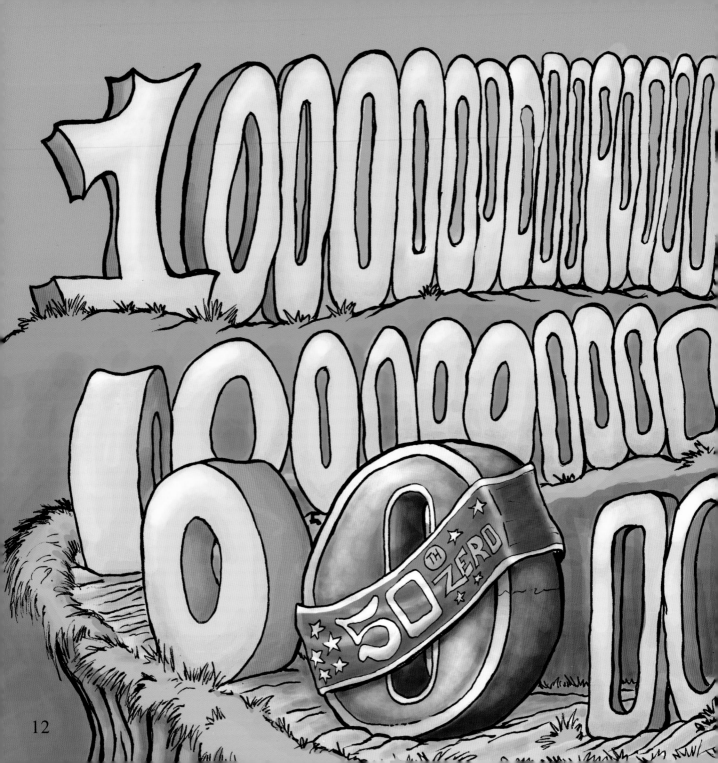

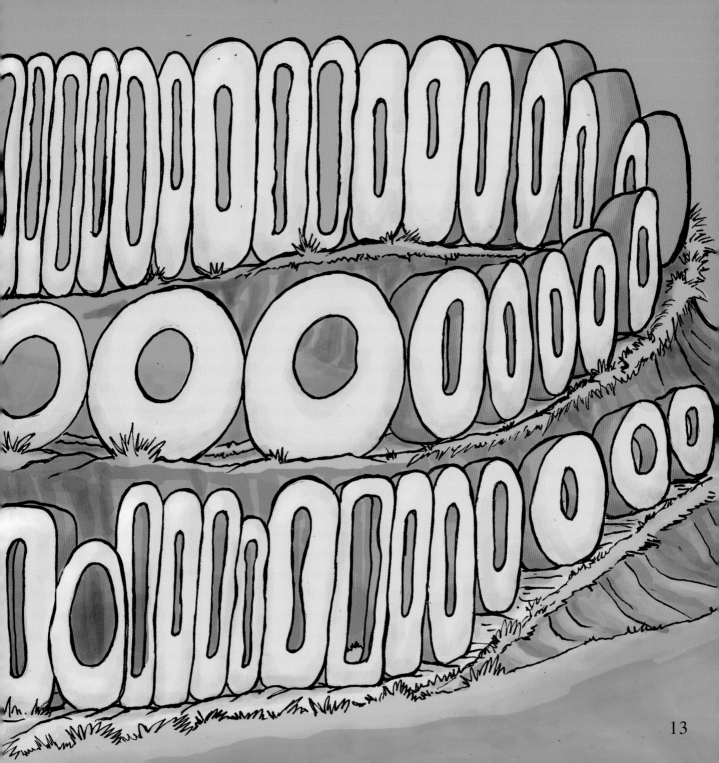

You write the number googol by writing a 1
followed by one hundred zeros.

How much is a googol?

It is more than a MILLION ,,,

more than a BILLION ,,,
and even much more
than a TRILLION.

A googol is more than almost anything you can imagine.

Just think of something there is a lot of.

A googol is more!

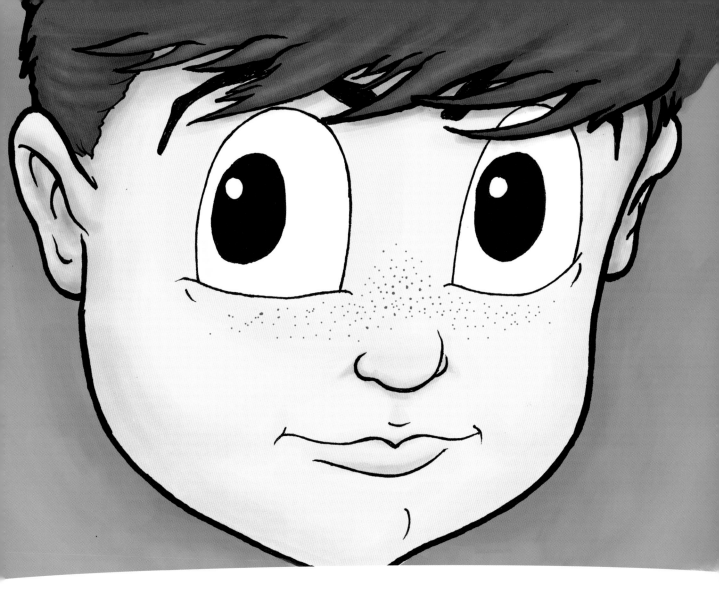

How many freckles are on
Anthony's face? A lot of freckles
but nowhere close to a googol.

If all the fans at a football game took off their shoes
and you counted their fingers and toes — not a googol.

1,496,060

In fact, you could measure every inch from
San Francisco to New York — less than a googol.

186,658,560

If you built a stack of pennies from your house to the moon, even to the sun, you would use fewer than a googol pennies.

1,253,440,000,000

To the sun

94,279,680,000,000

21

Just imagine a long Texas road full of fire ants,
one million ants wide, that stretches from
Texarkana to El Paso — not a googol fire ants.

825,200,640,000,000

How many seconds are in a year?

How many seconds are in a billion years?
Not a googol.

31,557,600,000,000,000

If the whole world was covered with grass —
no pavement, *no* concrete, *no* oceans — just grass,
still not a googol blades of grass.

790,653,726,720,000,000,000

If every inch of your backyard was covered
with postage stamps . . .

if the entire United States was covered
with postage stamps — not a googol stamps.

14,513,222,946,816,000

If you lined up hamburgers all the way from
Seattle to Miami and each burger had two pickles —

not even close to a googol pickles.

141,208,320

If every square foot in Washington, D.C., was covered with stacks of paper, and each stack of paper was 1,000 feet high (taller than the Washington Monument) . . .

and every piece of paper in those stacks
was covered with question marks,
you would not have a googol question marks.

36,883,123,200,000,000,000

Just how much is a googol?

A googol is more than Anthony's freckles,
more than the inches from
New York to San Francisco,
more than a stack of pennies to the moon,
more than a stack of pennies to the sun,
more than a road of fire ants across Texas,
more than the seconds in a billion years,
more than the question marks in Washington, D.C.,
and more than the pickles on hamburgers
from Seattle to Miami , , ,

PUT TOGETHER!

One day, Anthony finally reached his goal,
stopped counting, and proudly proclaimed,

"I COUNTED TO A GOOGOL!"

Uncle Stephen congratulated Anthony
and said, "There is a number much larger than a googol.
It is called a GOOGOLPLEX. You write a googolplex
by writing the number 1 followed by a googol zeros."

No one knows for sure if Anthony really counted
to a googol, but next time you see him acting quiet
and thinking to himself, don't bother him.

He might be trying to count
to a googolplex.

THE END

Googol really is a real number.

You may find it in the dictionary shortly after "goof-off" and "goofy." It has all the qualities of any other number – if you add one to it you get a googol and one; if you double it, you get two googol – but it is also unique. Most numbers are abstract and represent concrete objects. For example, the number 5 by itself is abstract, but we recognize that it can represent corresponding objects – 5 fingers, 5 children in a classroom, or 5 chairs. Googol, on the other hand, has no corresponding objects. It is purely abstract and as such, evokes pure imagination. For children, it is the perfect number.

Do you know anything there is a googol of?

Within the story, the numbers are obviously estimates – rounded off to the nearest one hundred million or so, but the calculations are based on mathematic principles.

The assumptions and calculations.

277 freckles
Anthony really does have a lot of freckles, but this is an estimate, perhaps exaggerated.

1,496,060 fingers and toes
Assumes every fan has 20 fingers and toes and the stadium capacity is 74,803.

186,658,560 inches
12 inches per foot; 5,280 feet per mile; 2,946 miles from San Francisco to New York.

253,440,000,000 pennies to the moon
Assumes 16 pennies per inch, 63,360 inches per mile, and 250,000 miles to the moon. The orbit of the moon means that the distance constantly changes, but 250,000 was a good number to use for the calculations.

94,279,680,000,000 pennies to the sun
Assumes 93,000,000 miles to the sun.

825,200,640,000,000 fire ants across Texas
Assumes 16 fire ants per inch; 63,360 inches per mile; 814 miles from Texarkana to El Paso; and 1,000,000 ants per row.

31,557,600,000,000,000 seconds in a billion years
60 seconds per minute; 60 minutes per hour; 24 hours per day; 365 ¼ days per year equals 31,557,600 seconds per year. Then, put nine zeros at the end to show a billion years.

790,653,726,720,000,000,000 blades of grass on Earth

Assumes 1,000 blades of grass per square inch and 196,950,000 square miles on Earth. This one is difficult with the square feet in a square mile (27,878,400) and the square inches in a square foot (144) multiplied by the square miles and by 1,000. This number can also be used to estimate the grains of sand. If the Earth was covered with a layer of grains of sand, 1,000 grains of sand per square inch, the number would be the same. To find the number of grains of sand if the sand is one billion grains of sand deep, simply add nine zeros to the end of the number. If a billion Earths are covered with sand a billion grains of sand deep, simply add nine more zeros. Still, not even close to a googol.

14,513,222,946,816,000 postage stamps

Assumes one stamp per square inch and 3,615,210 square miles in the United States.

141,208,320 pickles

Assumes the burgers are 3 inches wide; 3,343 miles from Seattle to Miami; and 2 pickles per hamburger. This number seems so small until you realize it is one hundred forty one million, two hundred eight thousand, three hundred twenty pickles.

36,883,123,200,000,000,000 question marks

Assumes two pieces of paper per square foot; 3,000 sheets of paper to form a stack of paper one foot tall; 63 square miles in Washington, D.C. 1,000 foot tall stacks; and 3,500 question marks per page.

827,583,840,477,036,179,217 put together

the sum.

Is there anything in the world that there is a googol of?

Yes. There are a googol numbers. I don't know of anything else.

So, is it possible for a child to count to a googol?

Of course, it is. Remember, no problem is so large that it can't be handled if you break it into manageable pieces.

Hint: Count by half googols.

You will arrive at a googol in no time.

Mark North Publications
1215 Gallatin Pike South
Madison, TN 37115